PIANO SHORTS

MEYARI MCFARLAND

CONTENTS

Other Books by Meyari McFarland:	v
Piano Shorts	1
Author's Note: Better With You	15
1. Goodbye, Hello	16
2. Old, New	24
Other Books by Meyari McFarland:	33
Afterword	35
Author Bio	37

PRAISE FOR MEYARI MCFARLAND

The rainbow has infinite shades, just as this collection covers the spectrum of fictional possibilities.

From contemporary romances like *The Shores of Twilight Bay* to dark fantasy like *A Lone Red Tree* and out to SF futures in *Child of Spring*, *Iridescent* covers the gamut of time, space and genre.

Meyari McFarland shows her mastery in this first omnibus collection of her short fiction. Twenty-five amazing stories, all with queer characters going on adventures, solving mysteries, and falling in love are here in the first Rainbow Collection.

And now you can get this massive collection of short queer fiction, all of it with the happy endings you love, *for free!*

Sign up here for your free copy of Iridescent now!

OTHER BOOKS BY MEYARI MCFARLAND:

Day Hunt on the Final Oblivion

Day of Joy

Immortal Sky

A New Path

Following the Trail

Crafting Home

Finding a Way

Go Between

Like Arrows of Fate

Out of Disaster

The Shores of Twilight Bay

Coming Together

Following the Beacon

The Solace of Her Clan

You can find these and many other books at www.MDR-Publishing.com. We are a small independent publisher focusing on LGBT content. Please sign up for our mailing list to get regular updates on the latest preorders and new releases and a free ebook!

Copyright ©2024 by Mary Raichle

Print ISBN: 978-1-64309-121-1

Cover image

[© Zeferli at DepositPhoto ID# 274348602](#)

All rights reserved. No part of this publication may be reproduced or transmitted in any form or by any means, electronic or mechanical, including photocopy, recording or any information storage and retrieval system, without permission in writing from the publisher.

Requests for permission to make copies of any part of the work should be emailed to publisher@mdr-publishing.com.

This book is also available in TPB format from all major retailers.

❀ Created with Vellum

This story is dedicated to my mom for making sure that my brother and I learned just enough music as kids. I was never very good at it, but I'm so glad I did get to learn.

PIANO SHORTS

The wind whistled in the eaves as Dale settled down at his battered old upright piano. It'd taken six people two hours to get it up the four flights to his apartment, but it was so worth every bruise, curse, and strained muscle. Leaves from the elm rustled like sheaves of paper, branches quickly going bare while tapping against the roof and the one window in his narrow little living room. Warm orange-red light shaded the key's golden where the ivory hadn't worn down to the point the underlying wood showed through like fingerprints left by time.

Grandma had always complained that the piano needed to be tossed out. She'd glare as Grandpa settled on the bench, winding it up three notches because the bench was as old as the piano, and it never stayed the right height. As Grandpa started playing, his arms would slowly rise until he was hunching over the keyboard instead of holding good posture.

"That thing is a hunk of junk!" Grandma would announce just as soon as Grandpa was done playing. "I don't know why you keep that thing around, you old fool. It's garbage."

"There's beauty in music," was all Grandpa would ever say as he cleaned the keys, returned the wires that had gone loose in the playing and then tucked the bench back into its place. He wasn't wrong. Even Grandma had known the truth: the piano might be old, but it still made beautiful music.

It was the one thing that Dale had wanted when his grandparents died. No one else contested him hauling the piano away. They were too busy fighting over the china, the silverware and who'd get which knickknack.

Dale hadn't kept the bench.

He hummed as he gentle began to play. Six notes later, Dale stopped, laughing, because wow, so much tuning he needed to do. If the piano could even be tuned. It might be like that old bench, too far gone for tuning to hold even though Grandpa had always been able to coax the piano into behaving just long enough for a song or two or three.

"Guess I'd best call someone in," Dale murmured as he ran his fingers over the worn keys.

He could've sworn the piano shivered with the memory of Grandpa's music, vibrating under his fingertips ever so faintly. Dale shut his eyes and let the long-ago music hum inside of his soul just the way it still hummed through the old piano. Maybe he could do the tuning himself?

Dale nodded slowly, then gave it a hard nod as he opened his eyes. Yeah, this time he'd give it a try. If it didn't work, well, no harm done. He could call someone in later. For now, for tonight, he'd rather tinker with his beautiful piano and see what he could accomplish alone.

Though playing for someone else was always better than playing for just yourself.

"Why do you play when Grandma gets so mean about the piano?" Dale had asked when his chin was just the height of the keyboard. "Why not play when she's not around to complain?"

Grandpa had laughed and ruffled Dale's hair, broad rough fingertips scratching against Dale's scalp. "I don't play for me, kiddo. The music, it comes from inside. It's the sharing that makes the beauty. Not my problem if your grandmother objects to the tool I use to make that beauty show, now is it?"

Dale had shaken his head back then. He stood, one hand on the keyboard and the other on the lid over the piano strings. Grandpa's piano was gorgeous, rich warm red wood carved with elaborate scrolls and reliefs. The craftsman had taken the time to put perfectly even fluting on the corners and gorgeous columns supporting the keyboard that looked like classical Greek vases. All the gold paint from the maker's mark had worn off two generations ago, before the piano even came to Grandpa.

"Right," Dale murmured as he opened the top of the piano and looked at the dozens of little tuning pins. "Let's see what I can do. Grandpa did it. No reason why I can't, too?"

KAMRYN SIGHED as he trudged up the stairs to his apartment. The old Victorian on the north side of Everett was a grand old lady in the truest sense, but damn it, he'd pay a ton of money right now to have an elevator instead of three flights of stairs to get to his apartment.

He was cold. He was tired. He wanted something to eat, a hot shower and then he'd collapse into bed. Nothing, but nothing was going to keep him from hiding under the covers.

As he unlocked his apartment door, piano music welled up across the hallway.

Kamryn frowned. Dale couldn't be back yet, could he? His grandmother'd just died. The funeral should've been two days ago. He would've thought that Dale would still be there dealing with his relatives.

But no, that was a real piano, not a radio on too loud. Kamryn winced as one of the notes went persistently off key. He shook his head and headed into his apartment, dumping his jacket on the old coat rack by the door, his shoes in a heap and his briefcase next to them. Groceries, what little he'd gotten, went into the fridge so he'd have lunch tomorrow. That only left dinner tonight.

Something simple. Something quick. And hot. Definitely something hot.

Kamryn's eyes crossed as he considered grilled cheese sandwiches, reheating soup, make frozen pizza. He did have one in the freezer, right?

No. No pizza. Oh yeah, he'd eaten that earlier in the week. Damn it, back to grilled cheese which felt like way too much work.

All the while, Dale played the piano across the hall.

Kamryn found himself pulling out bread, cheddar and some pre-sliced swiss he'd gotten and never used. None of it had mold so good enough. Oh, and there was some leftover deli ham.

"Okay then, grilled ham and swiss is good enough to make it worthwhile," Kamryn said.

The piano played on, bright and joyful despite the occasional off-key notes. Dale didn't sing as he played. Kamryn had never heard Dale sing, honestly, not even in the shower which was outright odd. Everyone sung in the shower, or at least everyone Kamryn knew did.

Or maybe that was just him.

He laughed and then winced as Dale hit a series of off-key notes that jangled in just the wrong way. It didn't seem to slow Dale down, though, because he swung into a bright

Ragtime that got right into Kamryn's toes, setting him to dancing as he grilled his sandwich.

It was the most natural thing in the world to start singing along, not that Kamryn really knew which Ragtime Dale was playing. Didn't much matter because Ragtime Gal's words fit just fine with the song that evened out as Dale played on. It was like Kamryn's singing soothed the out of tune keys or maybe Dale's playing smoothed out.

Either way, Kamryn sang until his sandwich was properly golden brown and melty, which was about the time Dale finally laughed and the music stumbled to a stop. Kamryn sucked in a breath and then laughed along with him as he gathered up his sandwich and a beer.

Sometime, this weekend maybe, Kamryn was going to bring a twelve-pack and a pizza so that he could sing properly as Dale played. For now though, his sandwich waited. Kamryn toasted Dale through the shut door before drinking.

He was kind of glad that Dale had escaped from his family and come home. No, make that really glad. Though Dale really did need to get those keys tuned up properly. Wow. So off-key.

ELLERY STRUGGLED to keep Sasha in her arms as Carrol opened their mailbox and fished out their latest stack of junk mail. Sasha, with full not-quite-two-year-old enthusiasm, squealed and made grabby hands at the stack of colorful flyers. It was a darn good thing that he was wearing his new winter jacket, or the kid would've taken a header into the hardwood floor as he dove for the flyers.

"No!" Ellery squawked as she grabbed Sasha's hood and hauled him back upright in her arms. "Come on, kiddo. Upright. That's it. Now you get the pretty paper."

Sasha squealed again as Carrol passed him one of the flyers. It was a thicker cardstock one that he wouldn't immediately shred into confetti. The rest of it would be destroyed pretty much the instant Sasha got his hands on it.

"That's not the reaction I'm used to when people get junk mail," said Dale, their upstairs neighbor with the gorgeous old piano. He grinned and waved at Sasha. "Happy?"

"Happy!" Sasha shouted, waving the flyer and smacking Ellery in the face with it.

"He loves him some junk mail," Carrol said, grinning as she grabbed their groceries from the floor. "Also loved your playing last night. He was dancing around in the living room."

"...No," Dale said, eyes going wide first and then wrinkling up as he grinned with delight.

"Oh, heck yeah," Ellery said. She wagged her eyebrows. "I filmed it. Between you and Kamryn singing, Sasha was in heaven. He loves music."

Dale blushed and rubbed the back of his neck before edging past Ellery to get at his mailbox. There were only six apartments in their old Victorian. Two up on the attic floor: Dale and Kamryn who really ought to get together finally. The two of them kept orbiting each other but not quite making contact. Maybe the piano would finally do it.

Ellery and Carrol shared an apartment directly below Dale's, a bigger three bedroom one instead of Dale and Kamryn's one-beds. The neighbor opposite them, Lorento, had helped with the piano and then swore that he was never, ever, on pain of death, doing something like that again.

"The out of tune keys weren't a problem?" Dale asked once he had his stack of junk mail plus about four bills out of his box.

"Nah," Ellery said. She spluttered and hauled Sasha back

in when he dove for Dale's junk mail. "It's fine. Kind of evened out towards the end of that bouncy bit you did. Like you shook the kinks out and everything got smooth, you know?"

Dale nodded though he looked kind of puzzled about it. "Yeah, I noticed that too. Anyway, I should head up. You have a good night. Bye-bye, Sasha!"

"Bye!" Sasha screeched, waving the flyer so hard that it flew right out of his pudgy little hand.

Both Ellery and Carrol snatched for it. The tantrum loomed, inevitable if Sasha thought his pretty flyer was gone for good, and for Sasha anything that wasn't in his line of sight was gone. Even if he got it back, he wouldn't realize it was the same flyer.

Dale whooped, grabbed and rescued the flyer before it could hit the floor.

Sasha hiccupped and then started clapping his hands wildly as if Dale had worked magic. When Dale handed Sasha the flyer, Sasha kissed it and then rubbed it all over his face. Ellery sighed. She was going to have to give Sasha such a bath. Hopefully, he wouldn't have another screaming fit about it this time.

"Night," Dale said without waving this time.

He ran up the stairs, leaving Ellery and Carrol to follow more slowly. As expected, Sasha turned all the junk mail into colorful confetti the instant they were in the house and the groceries were put away.

Dinner was a challenge. Sasha kept fussing, protesting the peas he'd adored yesterday and crying for the steamed asparagus that he'd loathed last week. Kids. Ellery was never, ever going to figure him out. Or, more likely, she'd figure him out just about the time he got enough words to explain what was going on in his head.

She'd take it.

As Carrol tried to clean Sasha's face and hands despite his squirming, incoherent wails of outrage that she'd strip off Sasha's wonderful coating of food and slobber, Ellery put the dishes in the dishwasher.

"He's so gonna need a…" Carrol didn't say "bath".

"Oh, I know it," Ellery agreed. "That's going to be a problem."

Sasha pouted and then started crying as if he'd heard the word "bath" despite neither of them saying it. Outright screams of outrage and heartbreaking wails like he was dying filled their apartment.

For all of about thirty seconds.

Then Dale started playing his piano upstairs. It wasn't that sprightly tune that bounced around the room like Sasha in his very best, brightest, happiest mood. This was a soothing song, like a lullaby, though Ellery didn't know it.

Sasha hiccupped and stared at the ceiling. He stuffed one still-grubby fist in his mouth and then held his arms out to Carrol to be picked up. Carrol did, kissing his forehead and swaying in time with the music that sounded like Ellery's mom humming, like waltzes with Carrol before they had Sasha, like cuddling under blankets and soaking in a nice warm…

"Bath time," Ellery declared. She wagged her eyebrows when Carrol winced. "Hear that, Sasha? It's bath time, baby!"

Stunningly, Sasha didn't pitch a fit as Ellery ran water in the tub. He didn't scream or cry getting his hair washed or his hands and face cleaned properly. He even let them dry him off, put on a new diaper, and then wrap him up in his favorite pink unicorn-bunny jammies.

"You think we could ask Dale to play something soothing every night?" Carrol whispered once they put Sasha down to sleep and he not only didn't fight but dropped off as soon as his head hit the pillow.

"Maybe," Ellery said, with a deeply relieved sigh. "We have got to make that man a cheesecake. A really big, really rich, really amazing cheesecake."

"This weekend," Carron agreed.

They both peeked in at Sasha who was at maximum cuteness with his jammies and his little face slack and peaceful as he snuffled and snored quietly. Yeah, they totally owed Dale a cheesecake, especially if he could play the piano and it had this affect again.

LORENTO FLOPPED ON HIS COUCH, eyes shutting out the world even though his mind would not shut up. Six audits that had to be done in the next two weeks, twelve documents that needed updates, four meetings tomorrow alone. He had no idea how he was going to get it all done. There simply wasn't enough time in the day.

It didn't help that he couldn't sort out which task needed to be done first. Well, no, he knew what needed the most attention: the audits. He had an entirely new batch of auditors. All of them needed supervision and training which meant that Lorento should set up a training schedule for each of them individually. They couldn't plan their audits so he would have to provide questions, encourage them to speak up during the audits, guide them through every step of the process.

Which was, in fact, what two of the meetings were about so it might be better to prepare for those first thing in the morning? No, not the meetings. The documents. The documents needed so much editing and they would be necessary for the audits. Lorento should have gotten the edits done months ago but there just hadn't been time.

He groaned and rubbed his hands over his eyes hard enough to make black and white kaleidoscope patterns bloom behind his eyelids.

Too much to do. Just too much to do and his brain would. Not. Stop!

The only time he'd managed to calm down enough to relax was when Dale had played his stupidly heavy and ridiculously out of tune old piano. The thing was a mess of jangling off-tune keys but somehow every night this week Dale had managed to make beautiful music.

Truly beautiful.

Not performance quality, certainly. Lorento had learned to play the piano as a child. His mother had driven him to be concert-quality until he'd threatened to take an ax to the damned baby grand as a teenager.

Dale had little to no training. It showed in the awkward chord progressions and his stumbling fingering when he tried to play the faster songs. His rhythm lagged in the beginning, sped in the middle, and then tended to settle towards the end of each song. Seriously, he was no pro. He didn't even qualify as a serious amateur.

And yet, when he played, there was a lightness and joy that allowed Lorento to overlook every single error, all the keys that weren't properly in tune. All the sagging and leaping, surging and limping timing didn't matter at all.

Because Dale played like he was pouring all the love of the world into every single song. He played...

Music echoed through the old Victorian. Dale's piano sounded grumpy tonight. Lorento stared up at the patched and water-stained ceiling. Something must have annoyed Dale because my goodness, he was hammering those delicate old keys.

Hard and fast, stumbling every time he tried to do a proper progression, Dale poured his anger into his piano and soon, stunningly soon, the music smoothed out. Lorento rolled off his couch, stretched until his spine cracked, and then went to pull the containers of Chinese out of his fridge. It was the work of three minutes to heat everything up.

By the time his microwave binged, Dale's music had shifted sad and lonely.

Lorento gathered up his take-out boxes and then knocked on Ellery and Carrol's door.

"He's not doing well today, is he?" Ellery said the instant she opened his door.

"Not at all," Lorento agreed. "I'm going to go share some dinner. The man doesn't eat half as much as he should."

Ellery blinked and then grinned. "We'll be right behind you. Carrol made an amazing goulash and I have this glorious apple pie we just baked yesterday. See if you can wake Kamryn up. He needs to flirt with Dale so badly."

She shut the door in Lorento's face, leaving him spluttering a laugh. Not that she was wrong. The UST between Kamryn and Dale was thick as cold gravy. Thankfully, Kamryn was in his apartment once Lorento headed upstairs to the top floor.

"We're invading," Lorento announced as Kamryn loomed in his doorway like a mountain made flesh. "Bring something to drink, napkins of some kind and help us distract Dale from whatever's upset him."

Kamryn started to say "who?" but then Ellery came up the stairs with Sasha in her arms and Carrol on her heels with a goulash wrapped in a blue bath towel and an apple pie that had a quarter cut out of it.

"...Okay then," Kamryn said, rugged eyebrows going right up to his hairline. "Let's do this."

His offering was a case of beer, a stack of napkins that

little Sasha grabbed for like they were the best toy ever, and a grin as he lightly kicked Dale's door.

Dale stopped playing.

Stomped over.

Opened the door and then stood there staring at them all with his mouth dropped open.

"We're invading," Lorento declared. "Move. We have food, dessert and Kamryn wants to kiss you senseless."

"I do not!" Kamryn squawked, going blazingly red as Lorento pushed right past him into Dale's perfectly neat little apartment.

"Of course you do," Lorento said.

Dale blushed just as violently as Kamryn, but he still let them in. He sat at his ridiculous old piano at first but when Lorento huffed and pushed him towards the couch where Kamryn sat with Sasha on one knee and a plate with mingled Chinese leftovers and goulash on the other, Dale went and sat and then smiled.

"This needs so much tuning," Lorento said.

"It's old," Dale said, shrugging. "You're welcome to try but the tuning pins slip quickly. I try to tune it up a bit every time I play, and it still slides out of tune."

Lorento huffed, put his plate in the kitchen and set to work on the piano. Behind him, the others chatted, told stories and laughed. So much laughter. At first it was mostly Ellery and Carrol but soon Kamryn was laughing with them. Sascha giggled and snuggled and draped himself over Dale's lap.

By the time Lorento had carefully, slowly, painstakingly tuned every single string of the piano, Dale was laughing with them all. Lorento smiled. Good.

"There we go," Lorento said as he shut the lid. "Come on now. Give us a tune, piano man."

"Oh God, I cannot believe you said that," Kamryn groaned.

"He's our piano man," Lorento said with a smile at Dale that made Dale blink and then smile like the sun coming out from behind storm clouds in the middle of winter.

"I guess I am," Dale said.

He switched places with Lorento, fingers caressing the old keys. Lorento settled back into the couch with Sasha bouncing by his knees. When Dale started to play, Sasha gasped and clapped his hands. Sasha danced, all toddler enthusiasm and with not a shred of self-consciousness.

Lorento leaned back in the sofa and let his eyes slide shut. So much joy.

DALE PLAYED. Not like Grandpa who played for Grandma and no one else. Not even like he'd played since he brought the piano home from his ungrateful relatives. No, this time he played for his neighbors.

The family he'd found.

His apartment smelled like food and sounded like laughter. It felt crowded instead of bare and quiet. And his music didn't echo in a room that was all sounding box instead of a place to live. The piano's song hit breathing, laughing, smiling bodies, warm and happy hearts, rebounding to bring their joy and love to Dale.

He played.

Laughed for Sasha's dancing.

Grinned for Ellery and Carrol's clapping.

Blushed for Kamryn's glorious singing voice once he came over to lean on the piano and stare into Dale's eyes as they made music together.

And smiled when he realized that Lorento had fallen asleep with a smile on his worn, tired face, the first Dale had ever seen there.

Dale smiled, turned back to his wonderful old piano, and played some more.

AUTHOR'S NOTE: BETTER WITH YOU

The little moments in life can carry you through trouble, loss, and fear. They can carry a marriage and make it strong, or break it apart when the two of you value different things. All those tiny little things that pass by unnoticed can be so very revealing of what you really care about.

Better With You is built around all those tiny moments, just like Piano Short. Building a life of your own after a divorce and finding yourself in the midst of chaos is always easier when you have someone who chooses to be by your side.

Hope you enjoy the sample!

1. GOODBYE, HELLO

Morgan wrinkled her nose as she hefted the last packing box. The thing smelled of mold. Not strong. But enough. Thank goodness it was leaving her apartment. Xiang had sworn up and down that the once-leaky window in the spare bedroom hadn't gotten anything wet but obviously she hadn't known what she was talking about. Whatever was in the box had definitely gotten moldy.

Her apartment was so empty now. Where there had been bookshelves full of Xiang's legal books and two huge sofas filling every spare inch of space, now there was open walls, slightly grey from lack of dusting, and so much floor space that Morgan felt like she could breathe for the first time in four years.

No more black leather sofa. That was going to be amazing. No big recliner sofa with fake brown suede, either. Xiang had already moved both of them to her new apartment across town. They looked a lot better there than they ever had in this apartment. It was suited for that sleek modern look that Xiang loved so much.

Old Victorians didn't do well with sleek and modern.

Neither had Morgan. If she never sat on another leather sofa it'd be way too soon. Especially in the summertime. Sticking to furniture was awful. And trying to cuddle on those things had been an exercise in frustration. They were too engineered, full of rigid beams under the stuffing that made cuddle time a struggle just to get comfortable.

Xiang had bought most of the furniture they'd shared, certain that they were destined for forever when Morgan was equally sure that nope, it wasn't going to last past college. The marriage hadn't been too bad, really. They'd made decent roommates.

Wives?

Not so much.

"That it?" Xiang asked, dust across her nose and sweat darkening her perfect linen shirt at the chest and armpit.

"Yep," Morgan said. "Last one. You've got dust on your nose."

"Gah, I swear I am taking an hour-long shower once I've got all of these in the apartment," Xiang complained. "I'm going to sweep the bedrooms and bathroom, make sure I didn't miss anything. You sure you don't want to keep some of the furniture, Em? Seriously, this place echoes now."

"I'm very sure," Morgan said so firmly that Xiang grinned at her. She really was adorable when she grinned that way, short and plump, hair pinned up so it spiked on the back of her head like an anime character. "I get the bed, you get the furniture. I'll be fine. After a good night's sleep, I'm going shopping for furniture for me."

"Good plan," Xiang said, heading on into the apartment.

By the time Morgan had loaded the last box into Xiang's moving truck, the littlest one you could rent that was actually a truck, Xiang was done. She had Morgan's purse and keys, which she passed over with a nod. Her nose was clean, too, which made Morgan grin.

"One more thing and you'll be done with me," Xiang said.

"Three things," Morgan said, snorting at her. "Unload the truck and turn it back in. Then drive you back to your apartment. So, yeah, maybe two hours. And seriously? You're never going to be done with me. We were wives. I get to meddle and gossip in eternity."

Xiang burst out laughing, hugging Morgan hard. She was strong for someone so small but then that was one of the things that'd attracted Morgan in the first place. If there was one thing that always drew Morgan in, it was strength. Strong minds, strong bodies, strong characters, didn't matter, it was catnip of the best kind.

It was more like three hours before Morgan dropped Xiang off at her apartment's front door. Nice place, all new construction with restaurants underneath sleek apartments on the upper levels. The parking garage and elevators were so new that Morgan had felt like she was going to be run out at any second in her battered old Ford pickup.

"Dinner?" Xiang suggested. And then yawned widely.

"Nah," Morgan said. She snorted at Xiang. "Seriously doubt you'll be awake more than a few minutes after you get inside. It's a good thing we made the bed up before we did anything else. Go on. Get some sleep and call me if you need anything, okay?"

"I will," Xiang promised without meaning it.

It showed in her formal little smile and the pat on Morgan's arm. Which was fine. Morgan didn't really mean the offer of help either, not unless it was something really huge. Lord knows, Xiang was probably going to be the one helping everyone else. She was the one with a law degree, after all.

Morgan was just muddling along with her silly little job and the quilts she made in her spare time.

They waved to each other and that was that. As Morgan

drove away, she was a little flummoxed at how easy it had been to let Xiang go. Shouldn't four years matter more? Dad had certainly been dismayed when Morgan called and told him that they were getting divorced.

"She's not cheating on you, is she?" Dad had asked, voice full of worry. Morgan had easily heard him tapping his fingers on the counter over the phone. He always did that when he worried himself to a frazzle.

"Dad, no," Morgan had groaned. "You know it was just a college thing. We got much better scholarships and stuff being married. It was never some big romantic thing. We're just going in different directions."

"But you loved her?" Dad had asked.

But he hadn't sounded confident about it at all. And frankly? Morgan couldn't blame him.

She'd never felt that all-consuming passion people talked about. Love had never, ever felt that way to her. It was small and calm and quiet. Gentle instead of fiery. Sure, Xiang had been a bit jealous at the beginning but after a few months she'd realized that no, Morgan literally wasn't looking at anyone else.

Marriage mattered. You had to take it seriously. That was just required. So Morgan had stopped flirting with other girls. She'd focused her attention and care on Xiang but somehow it had never been enough for Xiang. Choosing Xiang every morning and every night wasn't what Xiang had pined for and Morgan had seen the ending of their marriage in the beginning.

Their wedding vows had showed just how different they really were.

Love, honor and respect on Morgan's side versus eternal love of the ages on Xiang's. Not a great matchup there.

Their fights were never big screaming matches. They were little things. Xiang fretting about the furniture or finances. Morgan fussing over the floors getting vacuumed more than once every month. Whose turn it was to wash the dishes or fold laundry.

Just like any roommate Morgan had ever had.

And that, really, was what had driven them apart. At least that was what Morgan thought. When Xiang came to her after getting her Law degree and said that she wanted to get a divorce, Morgan had only blinked and nodded. There'd been no shock. No surprise.

They hadn't had sex for months before that so yeah.

Not a surprise.

A shame, really, but not a surprise.

She sighed once she made it back to her apartment. Frankly, Morgan wasn't all that sure she'd be awake much longer, either. They'd spread the moving out over a week but this last push had still ben brutal. Her whole body ached.

Morgan stood in the doorway of her apartment, studying the emptiness for a long moment before she shut the door. The little table she'd found at a yard sale stood by the front door. Perfect spot for her purse and keys. Her shoes fit underneath without a fuss. Much better than Xiang's insistence that they had to have a big wardrobe with black lacquer and frosted white glass sliding doors since the apartment had no coat closet.

Tomorrow, Morgan was going to buy some of those sticky-backed coat hooks, the ones that would hold twenty pounds. That'd suffice for a coat closet. And she was getting some pallets, a cheap twin sized mattress. She had that Guatemalan fabric, the red and purple striped stuff. That would make an excellent mattress cover.

"I can pull out all my pillow covers," Morgan said, starting to grin. "And my quilts. Oh! I can hang my quilts up again. I'm going to have to clean everything."

In the morning. Of course. Because she was sore and tired.

About ten minutes later, Morgan found herself in the spare bedroom rooting through the milk crates she'd used to store all her craft things. She hummed, spreading pillow covers and quilts all around her on the hardwood floors. Red and blue and green and yellow; all the colors of the rainbow. Man, she'd missed her art while married to Xiang.

It wasn't as though Xiang had forbidden Morgan from sewing. She'd given up the spare bedroom specifically so that Morgan had a place to work.

The problem had been that anytime Morgan sewed, Xiang had wrinkled her nose about the clipped threads. She'd huffed about the batting making dust. Had fussed over pins escaping the spare bedroom and migrating across the floor to where Xiang would cook her delicious traditional Mandarin dinners.

So Morgan had cut back on her sewing. Had done it when Xiang wasn't around. Then she'd sewed less and less until it was once a week instead of every day.

"We should have gotten a divorce much sooner," Morgan murmured as she smoothed her beloved lotus quilt over her thighs. The elaborate hand quilting dimpled under her fingertips. "I guess I didn't realize how much I was giving up to be with Xiang."

Sad.

How much had Xiang given up to be with Morgan?

A lot. Her favorite wines that Morgan couldn't drink without fear of a life-threatening migraine. The spicy food that made Morgan's stomach rebel until she sobbed. Late nights at clubs and her driving music that made Morgan shudder and turn away.

Yeah, their marriage really hadn't been one intended to last. As comfortable as they'd been together and as fond as

Morgan had been of Xiang, it was better for them to be divorced. Xiang had a bright career ahead of her. She'd take on the world and wrestle it into shape. Knowing Xiang, she'd find some lovely young intern, new at her firm, and seduce her right into Xiang's bed.

"I wonder," Morgan murmured as she got up, the lotus quilt in her arms. "Maybe I can make something appropriately sleek for Xiang to remember me with. A wall hanging, narrow. I bet she'd love it if I put that character, which was it? Love? No, Eternity. That was the one she loved."

Her design files were right there, tucked into old filing cabinets that Morgan had topped with a door that she'd covered with layers of wool blankets. On top of that she'd put a good cotton canvas so that she had a huge surface for pressing. Nothing but paperwork had touched that pressing table for so long.

Ridiculous.

Morgan hummed, her shoulders relaxing as she rooted through her files. Yes, Eternity, that was the character. Nicely graphic, complicated but not too hard to applique. She'd plan a wall hanging out tomorrow.

Though a quick sketch wouldn't hurt.

Morgan reached one hand out, batting around until she turned on her old radio, the one tuned to the classical music station. She smiled as a grand opera, no idea which one, came on. As Morgan started sketching, she sang along to the opera, making up her own words. Her lotus quilt stayed nicely draped over her shoulders like a cape the whole time.

Yeah, tomorrow she'd start her life over again.

"Or maybe," Morgan said with a laugh as she held up the sketch of a lovely new wall hanging that maybe, maybe not, would go to Xiang when it was done, "I'll start my life over again right now. So, do I want black and white or emerald and gold? What fabric do I have in my stash?"

She hummed as she headed back to the closet. They really should have divorced far sooner. Whenever Morgan got involved again, if she did, she wasn't giving up so much of herself. Not her art. Not again. It was far too important for her to let it go, even for a wife as beautiful and successful as Xiang.

2. OLD, NEW

Quinn put on her customer service smile, doing her best to ignore the pain in her cheeks, her shoulders, her poor abused feet. Stupid fifty percent off sale. Her boss was an asshole for making them all spend extra hours on his stupid promotion. But then, he never spent the day smiling at customers who alternated between painfully stupid and ridiculously abusive. Honestly, she couldn't remember the last time he'd spent more than five minutes in the store.

Asshole.

"Welcome to Furniture Barn," Quinn said to the dreamy-eyed woman who'd just walked in. "How can I help you?"

"Well, I was looking for several things," the woman said, holding up a scribbled-on piece of paper. "Pillows, particularly. But also a twin-sized mattress and box spring. Cheap is fine. It's for a day bed I'm making."

"Making?" Quinn asked, startled out of her customer service smile.

Just for an instant but that was more than long enough for customers to bitch to her boss about. Happened before, sure to happen again. Though maybe not today because the dreamy-eyed woman just nodded, a tiny little smile flickering about her lips.

"Oh yes," she said. "You see, I live in an old Victorian. I don't want something... formal, I suppose. I want a place to sprawl with lots of pillows and blankets. A day bed will work very well for that. And using pallets, well, that's just practical."

Quinn nodded, wondering just how long the woman had been out of college. Practical. Really. Last thing pallets were was practical when you could get a properly engineered day bed that would last for a decade or more.

"Well, we have some lovely day beds with built in storage," Quinn suggested. She gestured towards the back where the beds were kept. "That might take less work on your part than a bunch of pallets. Less potential damage to the floors, too."

"Oh, I hadn't thought of that," the woman said, blinking rapidly. She nodded once. "Hmm. Well, that's an interesting idea. Where are they?"

One of those, then. Quinn smiled just a little wider and led the woman back towards the beds. Or tried at any rate. The woman detoured to beam at a hanging lamp that looked like it'd just arrived from Marrakesh, then again for the aisle full of pillows, most of which were ugly as sin. Not that she seemed to give a damn what they looked like. Nope, she was more interested in hugging them and squishing them against her cheek.

"These are nice," the woman said once she'd gathered eight of them up in her arms, all squished and tumbled together there in a jumble that should have fallen the instant she breathed. They didn't. "I definitely want these. And that lamp. It's wonderful. Do you have more of them?"

"I... believe so," Quinn said far too warily for proper customer service. "They're different colors, not red."

"Perfect!"

Quinn's breath caught as the woman beamed at her. It was a damned good thing the boss wasn't around because Quinn would have gotten a writeup just for staring this way, not to mention everything else. Jeez, she hadn't had her heart trip over this way in ages. Frankly, she'd thought her heart and soul had both been surgically removed when she had to take this job. Sure felt that way, at any rate.

"The day beds are back here," Quinn said. "Are you looking for a more Bohemian style?"

"I'm... looking for homemade, crafted, super-comfortable, conglomeration of every style there is," the woman said. "I'm Morgan, by the way. I never like not knowing people's names. Or knowing theirs when they don't know mine. If everyone wore nametags that would be perfect."

Quinn swallowed a laugh, her fingers shaking a little as she smoothed her hands over her thighs. Her skirt's weave caught in her recently clipped nails.

"That would make like easier," Quinn said. "Thank you. And, of course, you can call me Quinn if you like."

"It's a very pretty name," Morgan said. Her smile was gentle now, though her eyes were still just as dreamy. "My ex-wife Xiang would have been so jealous of your name. She always wanted a 'normal' name."

Something locked up in Quinn's chest. She felt her smile go from 'customer service--delighted to see you' to 'locked up because brain is frozen'. Wife. Morgan had had a wife. Apparently one that she wasn't angry at or anything because there was no pain or fury in her eyes, her voice, as she said her ex-wife's name.

Damn.

A beautiful woman that Quinn could have a chance with, if only she wasn't working.

Just her luck.

Quinn pushed that away as firmly as possible. Job to do. Potential commissions to earn. Maybe, if she was very lucky, big commissions. That's what she needed to focus on so that's what Quinn would focus on. Not Morgan's lovely face or her full breasts or the way her hips rounded into full thighs that begged to be caressed.

Morgan gasped when she saw the day beds, tucked off to the side of the bedroom showing area. There weren't many of them, just four, all of them awkward crossbreeds of beds and sofas. Two of them were cast iron monstrosities that creaked as soon as you looked at them. One was a sleek platform bed set on top of stacks of three drawers that Quinn was absolutely certain would never, ever leave the store. It was ridiculously hard to pull the drawers and the back of the thing was so stiff that no one liked sitting on it.

"It's gorgeous!" Morgan exclaimed, shoving her stack of pillows into Quinn's arms with no warning.

She ran over to the fourth daybed, a huge chunky thing that had been crafted out of logs. Literal logs. It weighed a ton but it had shelves underneath the seat for storing baskets. Morgan climbed all over it, cooing as she tugged at the back and arms, bounced on the seat and then grinned as she flopped on the thing with her arms and legs flung out.

"Not what I expected you to choose," Quinn said. "That seems a bit rustic for a Victorian."

She walked over slowly only to drop the pillows around Morgan's head. Not on purpose. The pile of pillows was ridiculous and they got out of hand. Literally, but Morgan didn't seem to mind. She giggled and grinned up at Quinn.

"I did say I was looking for mismatched," Morgan said. "I want it. Does the mattress come with it?"

"It does," Quinn said. She pulled out her phone, scanning the tag on the bed. "Anything else you want? We offer free delivery and with this you're already over the limit."

Morgan sat up, sitting cross-legged on the day bed. She tilted her head to the side as if considering it. Or perhaps she was considering Quinn. Hard to tell. Those distant eyes didn't change at all.

"I do need a couple of comfortable chairs for guests," Morgan said. "And I need a small kitchen table with room for two. Something simple. Perhaps with stools."

Very profitable day if Quinn could find Morgan what she wanted. Days like this were why Quinn stayed instead of moving jobs. Commission on big purchases was always nice. It was the nickel and dime days that killed her.

"We've got all of that," Quinn said. "Plus blue, green and yellow versions of the lamp you liked."

Morgan gasped, beaming. "Show me!"

An hour later, Quinn waved as Morgan left with her four new lamps and fifteen new pillows, more having migrated into Morgan's arms as they shopped. The day bed, slipper chairs, coffee table and kitchen table with stools would all be delivered tomorrow. Come hell or high water, Quinn would see that they were delivered tomorrow because damn, Morgan had just paid off her outstanding credit card bill with one shopping spree.

People with money like that always amazed her. Ones with actual taste, those were rare. While every single piece that Morgan had picked was unique, they should all fit together beautifully. At least Quinn though they would. Other than the pillows. They were a weird conglomeration of colors and patterns that wouldn't fit together with anything at all, especially each other. But hey, maybe Morgan intended to get covers for them or something.

Not Quinn's problem.

Getting the delivery department to fulfill the company's promise to deliver next day (except holidays and during August when the boss was on vacation) was her problem.

"Rudo!" Quinn shouted once Placide finally showed up from her break. An hour after she'd gone for a ten-minute break, damn the woman. But this time it wasn't a problem. Meant that Quinn got every penny of the commission for Morgan's purchases and Placide didn't get a cent. Worked for her.

"What?" Rudo snarled at her from his desk tucked in beside the loading dock.

"I have a big order that needs to be delivered tomorrow," Quinn said. She shoved the order under his nose because otherwise he was going to pretend that he hadn't heard her. "Look at the total, Rudo. The boss will can your ass if we don't get it to the customer tomorrow. She's already said that she'd be home all day tomorrow but not for the rest of the week so we gotta deliver this."

"Great," Rudo grumbled. He took the slip and then frowned as he scanned down the thing. By the time he looked at the total on the bottom his eyebrows had flown up towards his grizzled hairline. "Okay, yeah, the boss will have my balls if we don't deliver this. She a repeat customer type or a one-off?"

"No idea," Quinn said. She snorted when Rudo glared at her. "She's one of the dreamers, Rudo. Smiling and gentle and a million miles away. She could come back every week for the next year or she could forget that we even exist. But giving her a reason to remember us should help. So, can we get these to her tomorrow morning?"

Rudo grumbled something under his breath that was sure to be profanity in at least three languages that Quinn didn't speak but he pulled out his schedule and nodded as he tapped the morning slots.

"We got an opening," Rudo said. "How many stairs we dealing with? That day bed is heavy as hell. She... huh, she paid for assembly, too. Nice."

"One story up," Quinn said, daring to lean her hip against Rudo's desk despite his hatred for people doing that. "Shouldn't be an issue. She said all the doorways are standard sizes. Apparently, her ex-wife had big sofas in there and they got in and out without any major problems."

Rudo stared at Quinn, blinking over the ex-wife just as hard as Quinn had wanted to. But then he'd never been a customer service worker. Delivery, procurement, accounts, that was Rudo. Not smile until your face fell off while your feet stabbed you with every step.

Lucky bastard.

"Huh. Right. Well, we can get it to her between eight and ten tomorrow," Rudo said. "Should I tell the guys to expect tips?"

"Tips, right. Good one." Quinn snorted a laugh that Rudo grinned at. "I'm going to go take an actual ten-minute break. Let me know if anything changes, okay?"

"Will do," Rudo said. "Scat, kiddo. Take a load off in the break room.

Broken room, really. The boss had never seen the point of putting in a proper break room for the employees so they just had a corner of the back warehouse where the broken things were stored pending repair to sit and relax for a bit. Placide was prone to taking naps back there but all Quinn ever did was sit, groan as her feet went pins and needles, and eat lunch.

And sketch.

The one holdover of her dreams. Quinn settled into the not quite fixed orange recliner that no one would ever fix because no one wanted to give up the most comfortable seat in the house. She pulled out the little notepad that she kept in her pocket all day and smiled.

A round, full face. Hair that drifted around her head like a cloud, brown and gently waving. Large eyes that saw things a thousand miles away. A snub nose. Lips so lush that they were made for kissing. Adorable double chin.

Morgan was gorgeous. Seriously, just stunning beautiful. And damn if she wasn't that hard to capture on paper. Not as good as it could have been if Quinn had the time and energy to sketch more but after a day of work the last thing she wanted was to spend time working on her art. All she wanted was to collapse.

Sometimes eating was too much effort after work.

Art was right out.

But today, now, Quinn found herself making eight or so quick sketches of Morgan's lovely face so that she wouldn't forget what she'd looked like. The beaming smile. Those giggles. The way she'd sprawled across the log daybed, arms and legs akimbo.

"Huh, you got it bad," Rudo said. He cackled as Quinn started so hard she dropped her pencil. "Man, I never sneak up on you. You really are smitten, aren't you?"

"Smitten," Quinn said, fishing around until she found her pencil. "Jeez, we're not in some stupid Regency Romance, dude. What's up? I still have… one whole minute of break."

Rudo rolled his eyes. "Yeah, yeah, whatever. Checked with the boys and Cyan's not going to be in tomorrow. According to Golshan, he's already snockered. You know he won't make it work if he's drunk off his ass tonight."

"That asshole!" Quinn groaned and glared up at Rudo who just stared back down at her. "Damn it. All right, you need help moving things?"

"Yup," Rudo said. "Golshan's tough but he's still only five four, Quinn. I can keep Placide on duty, not let her take her break, if you can go out with him to deliver the goods."

"Just that one run and we've got a deal," Quinn said. She wagged a finger at him. "No way am I going back to mover. I got out of that and I'm not getting back into it."

"Deal." Rudo wagged a thumb towards the front. "Now scoot. Placide called back that there's a family looking for kid beds and she's got some little old lady looking for a sofa her cat won't shred."

Quinn sighed. "On it. Thanks, Rudo. I appreciate it. So much."

He grinned at the sarcastic tone, patting her shoulder in that mock-fatherly way that said that he so felt her pain. Not.

"You're welcome, kiddo. Now move. We got a business to run here, no matter what Placide thinks."

Quinn went. At least tomorrow she'd get to see Morgan again. And she had the commission from today's work. It was all good. Good enough, anyway.

Time to get back to work.

Better With You is now available at all major retailers in ebook and TPB format.

OTHER BOOKS BY MEYARI MCFARLAND:

Day Hunt on the Final Oblivion

Day of Joy

Immortal Sky

A New Path

Following the Trail

Crafting Home

Finding a Way

Go Between

Like Arrows of Fate

Out of Disaster

The Shores of Twilight Bay

Coming Together

Following the Beacon

The Solace of Her Clan

You can find these and many other books at www.MDR-Publishing.com. We are a small independent publisher focusing on LGBT content. Please sign up for our mailing list to get regular updates on the latest preorders and new releases and a free ebook!

AFTERWORD

I've lived in the Puget Sound since 1997. To me, it feels like just a couple of years. It hurts my soul to realize it's been twenty-six years. Time flies when you're not paying attention.

That said, the Puget Sound has become it's own character in my stories. The rain, the grey winters and sunny hot summers; it's all there under my fingertips when I start writing. The traffic and the sunrises streaking the clouds gold and scarlet well up whenever I start a new story. I probably shouldn't be surprised. When a place becomes your home, it becomes a part of you at the same time you become a part of it.

That's what home is, isn't it?

If you want more stories like this one, please go sign up for my newsletter on www.MDR-Publishing.com. You'll get updates on whatever I've got coming up, special deals and you can get a free ebook or collection of my short stories. Or you can sign up at my Patreon and get access to my art, writing and whatever's going on creatively in my life.

Thank you for reading!

Meyari McFarland
February, 2024
www.MDR-Publishing.com

AUTHOR BIO

Meyari McFarland has been telling stories since she was a small child. Her stories range from adventures appropriate to children to erotica but they always feature strong characters who do what they think is right no matter what gets in their way.

Meyari has been married for twenty years and has no children or pets. She lives in the Puget Sound, WA and enjoys the fog, rain and cool weather that are typical here. When vacation times come, she and her husband usually go somewhere warm like Hawaii or they go on their own adventures to Japan and other far away countries.

Her life has included jobs ranging from cleaning motel rooms, food service, receptionist, building and editing digital maps, auditing and document control.

MORE FROM MEYARI MCFARLAND

Website:

. . .

MEYARI MCFARLAND

www.MDR-Publishing.com

SOCIAL MEDIA:

Patreon - https://www.patreon.com/meyarimcfarland
   Mastodon – https://wandering.shop/@MeyariMcFarland
   Pillowfort - https://www.pillowfort.social/Meyari
   Facebook   -   https://www.facebook.com/meyari.mcfarland.5
   Pinterest - https://www.pinterest.com/meyarim/

If you enjoyed this story, please leave a comment on your favorite site. Also, please sign up for the newsletter so that you can hear about the latest preorders and new releases.

www.ingramcontent.com/pod-product-compliance
Lightning Source LLC
LaVergne TN
LVHW042004060526
838200LV00041B/1866